Samuel French Acting Edition

Dani Girl

Music by
Michael Kooman

Book and Lyrics by
Christopher Dimond

DANI GIRL was given its world premiere at the Talk is Free Theatre Company at the Barrie Community Health Center in Ontario, Canada on January 29, 2011. The performance was directed by Richard Ouzonian, with sets and costumes by Christine Barrett, lighting by Gareth Crew, and musical direction by Wayne Gwillim. The Production Stage Manager was Pamela Craig. The cast was as follows:

DANI	Gabi Epstein
MOTHER	Jayme Armstrong
MARTY	Jonathan Logan
RAPH	Jake Epstein

DANI GIRL was originally presented as a workshop production at Carnegie Mellon University in 2007. It was further developed at American Conservatory Theatre, the ASCAP/Disney Musical Theatre Workshop, and CAP-21.

This play was presented as a staged reading in April 2008, at the John F. Kennedy Center for the Performing Arts, as part of New Visions/ New Voices.

DANI GIRL was presented at the National Alliance for Musical Theatre's Festival of New Musicals in 2011. www.namt.org

CHARACTERS

DANI – (9) Lively but morbid. Extremely imaginative. Precocious. May be played by an adult actress.

RAPH* – (Ageless) Dani's imaginary friend and guardian angel. Sarcastic but caring. Playful on cue. Appears as many other characters.

MARTY – (10) Odd and intelligent, bordering on dorky. Obsessed with movies. May be played by an adult actor.

MOTHER – (Late 30s) Dani's mother. Stern. Hard. Does what she believes is right to save her daughter and makes no apologies for it.

CANCER* – (Timeless) A chronic and terminal disease. Revels in being sinistern and malicious. Appears in several forms.

GOD* – (Eternal) Supreme being and all-powerful creator of the universe. Simple, straightforward, and comforting.

FATHER* – (35) Dani's father. Appears only in dream sequences.

An asterisk (*) denotes doubling.

SETTING

Children's Hospital of Pittsburgh. But mostly Dani's imagination.
Fall of 1990 through Spring of 1991.

For Daniel

(At rise: in black, singing.)

*[MUSIC NO. 01: **INVOCATION**]*

DANI.
> REQUIEM ETERNUM.
> REQUIEM ETERNUM.
> BENEDICTUS LACRIMOSA.

> *(Lights up to reveal **DANI**, placing a stuffed rabbit into a shoe box coffin.)*

> Dearly beloved. We are gathered to bid farewell to our esteemed friend, Sir Floppy McFloppersby.
> DIES IRAE. BUENOS DIAS.

> *(She places a bouquet of dandelions on his coffin.)*

> Forsooth! Sir Floppy was a noble stuffed rabbit, unlike his ancestors: the prideful Bugs Bunny, the lecherous Trix Rabbit, and that notorious abuser of field mice, Little Bunny Foo Foo. Behold, I say unto thee –

> *(enter **RAPH**, wearing pink wings)*

> What are you doing here?

RAPH. Paying my respects to Mr. McFloppyface.

DANI. It's Sir Floppy McFloppersby. And you didn't even know –

RAPH.
> DIES IRAE.

DANI. You can't expect to just waltz in here –

RAPH.
> DOMINOSA.
> PIZZAREIA.

DANI. That doesn't even make sense.
> DIES IRAE.

RAPH.
DIES IRAE.

DANI.
CORPUS CHRISTI.

RAPH.
CORPUS CHRISTI.

BOTH.
CHRISTIE BRINKLEY.
ET SPAGHETTIUM.

DANI. Yea, when Sir Floppy was taken from yon cruel world –

RAPH.
SNUFFLEUFAGUS.

DANI. Though he walked through the valley of the shadow of Mr. McGregor –

RAPH.
FRAGGLEROCKIUM.

DANI. He feared neither the cold clutch of death, nor the black grip of the grave.

RAPH.
MI SAY RE RE RE RE RE RE RE EXCELSIS!

DANI. Raph!

RAPH. Yes?

DANI. You make a terrible mortician.

RAPH. Sorry, morbid little funeral games aren't exactly my specialty.

DANI. I don't need you.

RAPH. Right, this is perfectly normal nine year old behavior.

DANI. I don't need a stupid guardian angel.

RAPH. *(reading from list)* Sir Floppy McFloppersby: one count malignant melanoma. Admiral Flounder Fishyfin: one count osteogillcoma, two counts dorsal sarcoma. Baron von Lemurstein –

DANI. What's your point?

RAPH. One by one you've been diagnosing your stuffed animals with –

DANI. I have been doing no such thing.

RAPH. Until the only one who's managed to escape unscathed is –

DANI. What's that, Mr. Fritz?

RAPH. Oh jeez.

(**DANI** *listens to her teddy bear.*)

*[MUSIC NO. 01A: **MR. FRITZ TALKS**]*

DANI. You're right, Mr. Fritz, we don't have time to talk to any second rate angels.

RAPH. Kiddo –

DANI. We're in the middle of a game. *(offering)* Raph?

RAPH. Sorry, I left my formaldehyde upstairs.

DANI. It's not funeral.

RAPH. No? Then what's the game?

DANI. Life. You can take Floppy's place. He wasn't very good.

RAPH. Evidently not.

DANI. Just shut up and play.

(*They begin to play a life-sized version of The Game of Life. They spin, read from cards, and move around the board.*)

*[MUSIC NO. 02: **THE GAME OF LIFE**]*

DANI. *(cont.)*
IN THE GAME OF LIFE,
YOU HAVE TO KNOW HOW TO SPIN.
IN THE GAME OF LIFE
YOU SIMPLY NEVER GIVE IN.
IN THE GAME OF LIFE
YOU HAVE TO KNOW HOW TO WIN.

(**DANI** *spins.*)

One, two, three.

(*reads card*)

DANI. *(cont.)*
> STUFFED RABBIT DIES OF A RARE DISEASE.
> SIX FEET DOWN OLD FLOPPY NOW DECAYS.
>
> *(turns card over)*
>
> AS PART OF HIS LAST WILL AND TESTAMENT
> HE LEAVES YOU ALL HIS MILKY WAYS.
>
> IN THE GAME OF LIFE,
> IF YOU SHOULD LOSE A GOOD FRIEND.
> IN THE GAME OF LIFE
> ON ONE THING YOU CAN DEPEND.
> THAT THE GAME OF LIFE
> WILL TURN OUT RIGHT IN THE END.
> Your turn.
>
> *(He spins.)*

RAPH, Christ's apostles minus Snow White's dwarves.

DANI. That's five.

RAPH. I know.

> *(He moves, then reads the card.)*
>
> CONGRATS! YOU'VE JUST WON THE NOBEL PRIZE.
> YOU FOUND THE CURE TO THE COMMON COUGH.
> BUT YOU CATCH A RARE FORM OF LEPROSY.
> AND YOUR LOWER LEFT LEG FALLS OFF.
> Surely you jest.

DANI. Rules are rules.

> *(He sighs and stands on one foot.)*
>
> LIFE IS CHUTES AND LADDERS.
> LIFE IS SORRY AND SPREE.
> LIFE IS LOTS OF HERSHEY KISSES.
> FOR FOLKS LIKE MR. FRITZ AND ME.

RAPH.
> IN THE GAME OF LIFE,
> IT ALL DEPENDS ON THE DEAL.
> IN THE GAME OF LIFE,
> SOMEHOW I CAN'T HELP BUT FEEL

THAT THE GAME OF LIFE
IS JUST A TRIFLE UNREAL.

DANI. Don't be bitter, Raph.

LIFE IS TWISTER AND CUPCAKES.

RAPH.

LIFE IS BLISTERS AND HEADACHES.

DANI.

LIFE IS BATTLESHIP AND NERDS.

RAPH.

LIFE IS BROCCOLI AND TURDS.

DANI.

LIFE IS HUNGRY, HUNGRY HIPPOS.

RAPH.

LIFE IS MOLDY FEET.

DANI.

WATCH MR. FRITZ AND LEARN.

(She spins.)

IN THE GAME OF LIFE
SOME PLAYERS NEVER GIVE IN.

RAPH.

IN THE GAME OF LIFE,
SOME LOSE ON EVERY SPIN.

DANI.

IN THE GAME OF LIFE –

RAPH.

IN THE GAME OF LIFE –

BOTH.

IN THE GAME OF LIFE –

RAPH.

SOME PEOPLE NEVER –

DANI.

SOME PEOPLE ALWAYS

BOTH.

WIN!

DANI. You see, Raph, you just have to look at things from
the proper – *(She reads the card.)* Oh dear.

RAPH. What is it? What does it say?

DANI. Teddy bear gets ovarian cancer. Oh, Mr. Fritz.

RAPH. Listen, it's time you and me had a heart to heart.

DANI. I haven't seen you for three years, Raph. Where've
you been?

RAPH. I do have other cases, you know. And besides, you
haven't needed me.

DANI. I don't need you now.

RAPH. Dani Lion, take a look around.

(The lights come up to reveal the hospital.)

What are we doing back here?

DANI. It's just a check up.

RAPH. You know better than –

DANI. There is nothing –

RAPH. Kiddo, you can talk to me. What's wrong?

DANI. I don't know.

RAPH. How do you feel?

DANI. I'm tired, Raph. I'm really tired.

RAPH. And you think that might mean –

DANI. I'm tired all the time. And now Mother disappears
with the doctors and tells me to stay here and play and
I can barely even stay a – *(she yawns)* I can barely even
stay –

[MUSIC NO. 02A: **DREAM SEQUENCE 1***]*

(The dream begins. **RAPH** *becomes* **FATHER,** *he holds a
baby.)*

FATHER. Once upon…

DANI. I can't even stay a –

(enter **MOTHER,** *in dream mode)*

MOTHER. Once upon…

DANI. Mother?

FATHER. Once upon a time.

DANI. Daddy?

FATHER. In the Kingdom of Blue Skies.

MOTHER. There lived a noble king, King William the Lionheart.

FATHER. With his elegant bride, Queen Katharine, the Compassionate. And one day,

MOTHER. As the sun rose high over their castle…

FATHER. They were blessed with a radiant…

MOTHER. A beautiful…

FATHER. A perfect…

BOTH. Daughter.

FATHER. They named her Danica Lyons, Princess of the Dandelions.

MOTHER. For she was as wild…

FATHER. And fearless…

MOTHER. And strong as a lion.

FATHER. And they all lived happily…

MOTHER. Happily…

BOTH. Happily ever after.

(*music out*)

(**DANI** *wakes up.* **FATHER** *and the baby disappear.*)

DANI. Mother?

MOTHER. Oh. You're awake?

DANI. Where am I?

MOTHER. Here. Take these.

DANI. I'm still in the hospital?

MOTHER. We have to get some tests –

DANI. Were you crying?

MOTHER. Just take the meds.

DANI. Mother? It's back again, isn't it?

(beat)

MOTHER. Dani…yes. It is.

DANI. No.

MOTHER. We've had three good years. We have to stay positive.

DANI. Will you tell me a story?

MOTHER. Once upon a time there was a little girl who wouldn't take her meds, and she never got ice cream for dinner again.

DANI. No, like you and Daddy used to tell.

MOTHER. Dani – don't.

DANI. But why?

MOTHER. Cinderella and Snow White, they could just sit around and wait for their princes, or fairy godmothers to save the day. You and I don't have that luxury, do we? All we've got is what's real. Here.

*(She takes out a religious medal on a chain and puts it around **DANI**'s neck.)*

Remember St. Raphael? The angel of healing?

*(enter **RAPH**, eating)*

RAPH. Sweet mother of mercy, the food in this place is positively revolting.

DANI. Unfortunately.

MOTHER. Hey, he got us through once, didn't he?

RAPH. Every time I'm here I think it can't have gotten worse.

DANI. I guess.

MOTHER. We are going to do whatever it takes.

RAPH. And yet every time…

MOTHER. And God will see us through again.

RAPH. The tapioca proves me wrong.

DANI. Can I have some cookies?

MOTHER. You haven't had breakfast.

   (**DANI** *smiles sweetly.*)

   Take the meds.

   (*She does.*)

   I spoil you child, I swear I do.

   (*She exits.*)

RAPH. What's with you?

DANI. I thought I was done.

RAPH. Hey, kid. It's not the end of the world.

DANI. I hate this place, Raph.

RAPH. C'mon.

DANI. It reeks of disease.

RAPH. (*looking at her chemo pole*) Look at all the cool stuff.

DANI. There's nothing cool about leukemia.

RAPH. Think of the games we can play.

DANI. I don't want to.

   (**RAPH** *becomes flamboyant French hairdresser* **RAPHAEL.***)*

   [*MUSIC NO. 02B:* **RAPHAEL'S SPA DE BEAUTY BEAUTY SPA**]

RAPHAEL. *Bonjour!*

DANI. I said –

RAPHAEL. Et welcome to Raphael's Spa de Beauty Beauty Spa.

DANI. I'm not playing.

RAPHAEL. Oh la la. Zis must be mademoiselle Danica, ze most *tres, tres, tres, belle femme* in ze world.

DANI. Well, perhaps one game.

RAPHAEL. *Bonne. Zut alors!*

DANI. What?

RAPHAEL. What is zis collection de stringy fungus on top of your 'ead?

DANI. My hair?

RAPHAEL. *Oui.* If zat is what you call 'air. It look like what you pull out of ze drain of une Turkish bath.

DANI. I like my hair.

RAPHAEL. *Mais non.* Zis will not do at all. But, never fear, *mademoiselle.* Nozing is too great a miracle for Raphael, 'airdresser to ze star.

(He shaves her head.)

Sacre bleu.

DANI. What?

RAPHAEL. *C'est magnifique.*

DANI. Let me see.

RAPHAEL. *C'est parfait.*

DANI. I want to see.

(He hands her a mirror.)

RAPHAEL. *C'est tres, tres, tres belle, non?*

(She sees herself).

DANI. No.

RAPHAEL. Pardonnez moi?

DANI. No.

RAPHAEL. Mais oui. It say beauty. It say strength. It say powerful woman at 'er very essence.

(music out)

DANI. It says sick.

RAPHAEL. You American –

DANI. I don't want to play anymore!

RAPH. Kid, there are some games you can't exactly quit.

DANI. Give me my hair back.

RAPH. That's not the way it works.

DANI. Oh yeah?

(She sits and concentrates.)

RAPH. What are you doing?

DANI. Growing back my hair.

RAPH. Kid, please. That's ridiculous.

(*pause*)

You know how this goes.

(*pause*)

Alright. Fine. You win.

DANI. (*opening one eye*) What?

RAPH. New game.

DANI. I'm listening.

(**RAPH** *becomes a pair of talk show hosts. He switches between* **WINK** *and* **CHANDRELLE.**)

[*MUSIC NO. 03:* ***TRIVIAL PURSUIT OF DEATH***]

WINK. Good evening, ladies and gentlemen. I'm Wink Winkendale, and this is Trivial Pursuit…of Death.

CHANDRELLE. It certainly is, Wink.

WINK. Thank you, Chandrelle.
TRIVIAL PURSUIT OF DEATH.
TRIVIAL PURSUIT OF DEATH.
SIT ON THE EDGE OF YOUR SEAT.
FEEL YOUR HEART BEAT.
WAIT WITH BAITED BREATH.
FOR TRIVIAL PURSUIT…
TRIVIAL PURSUIT…
OF DEATH.
Alright, let's meet our first contestant. All the way from pediatric oncology, let's give a warm welcome to Danica Lyons.

CHANDRELLE. That sure is a stylish hairstyle, Wink.

WINK. It certainly is, Chandrelle. Now Danica, here's how our game works: I'm going to ask you the six questions on this card. If you can answer all six correctly, you win some fantastic prizes. Tell her what she wins, Chandrelle.

CHANDRELLE. Her hair, Wink. She's playing for her hair.

WINK. Well, isn't that terrific, folks? And if she loses?

CHANDRELLE. Ooh, it's gonna be a long and drawn out treatment period full of pain and suffering, followed by almost certain death.

WINK. Let's not dwell on that, shall we? She's playing for her hair. Alright, our first category is blue, that's geography. Are you ready, Danica?

DANI. I suppose so.

WINK. Your question is…which constellation, drawn from the mythological creature that joined the Hydra in a fight against Hercules, is named for the Latin word for crab?

DANI. Cancer?

WINK. That is correct. Next question, green. Osteosarcoma, mesothelioma, astrocytoma, medulloblastoma, adrenal cortical carcinoma, and liver cancer are all types of what disease?

DANI. Cancer.

WINK. Correct again. Brown. Now, Danica, pay close attention. Henry Miller's 1934 sexually explicit novel is titled Tropic of what?

DANI. Cancer.

WINK. Unbelievable, ladies and gentlemen. This kid is on a roll. Danica, you are that much closer to getting your hair back. How do you feel?

DANI. Good.

WINK. That is correct. Are you ready for your next question?

DANI. Yes.

WINK. Correct again. Pink, entertainment. Known to be both healing and sensitive, what is the zodiological sign of individuals born between June 22nd and July 22nd?

DANI. Cancer!

WINK. That is once again correct. Yellow. History. Sixteenth President of the United States Abraham Lincoln did not die of what disease?

DANI. Cancer!

WINK. He certainly did not. Danica, only one question stands between you and your hair. Before we get to that question, let me ask you this: If you do answer correctly, what are you going to do with all that hair?

DANI. I don't know, Wink. I'll probably just brush it.

WINK. Brush it. Isn't that terrific folks? Alright, Danica. Are you ready?

DANI. Yes I am, Wink.

WINK. Then here it goes. For a lifetime supply of your own hair. The category is orange. And your question is… why is cancer?

DANI. What?

WINK. Why is cancer?

DANI. That's not fair.

WINK. Ten seconds, Danica.

DANI. It's not fair.

WINK. Five seconds.

DANI. I –

WINK. Three – two –

DANI. I…

WINK. I'm going to have to ask you for an answer, Danica.

DANI. I don't know.

WINK. Ooh. I'm sorry, that is incorrect. "I don't know" is not why cancer is. Tell her what she's won, Chandrelle… on second thought, don't tell her what she's won.

DANI. Raph.

WINK. That's all the time we have for today. So, until next time –

DANI. Raph!

(music out)

RAPH. What?

DANI. It's not fair.

RAPH. I'm sorry.

DANI. It's not even a real question.

RAPH. Hey, how are you supposed to get rid of something when you don't know why it's there?

DANI. I guess. It's just…Raph?

RAPH. Yeah, kid?

DANI. I don't want to…

RAPH. You want to be cured?

DANI. I want my hair back.

RAPH. I know. So, answer the question.

DANI. But I don't know.

RAPH. Then I guess you'd better find out.

(He exits. Enter **MOTHER.** *)*

MOTHER. Oh Sweet Jesus.

DANI. Don't.

MOTHER. My beautiful baby.

DANI. Why is this happening again?

MOTHER. I don't know.

DANI. It's gone.

MOTHER. I wish I did.

DANI. It's all gone.

MOTHER. But God…God has a plan. And for reasons that are beyond our understanding, that plan involves beating this again. So that is exactly what we are going to do. We are going to beat it for good.

DANI. How?

MOTHER. You're going to finish your chemo. And we are going to pray.

DANI. If prayer's so great, why do we need chemo?

MOTHER. The Lord helps those who help themselves.

DANI. Really?

MOTHER. C'mon, get your rosaries. In the name of the father, and of the son, and of the holy spirit…

*[MUSIC NO. 04: **MY HAIR**]*

DANI.

I'M NOT QUITE TEN.
YET ONCE AGAIN,
I'M STANDING FACE TO FACE WITH STUPID CANCER.

I BEAT HIM BEFORE
BUT NOW I'M UNSURE.
CAN I FIND A CURE IF I FIND YOUR STUPID ANSWER?

IF I FIND OUT WHY
THEN I WILL NOT DIE.
I'M GONNA FIND THE REASON IT'S THERE,
I'M GONNA GET BACK MY HAIR.

IN LIFE YOU LEARN
TO JUST SIT BY.
BUT I'M SICK AND TIRED OF BEING SICK AND TIRED.
I'M SO APPALLED,
BY BEING BALD.
SO I'M RESOLVED, YES NOW I AM INSPIRED.
THIS TIME IT'S DO OR DIE.
CANCER, SAY GOODBYE.
TRY TO STOP ME IF YOU DARE,
I'M GONNA GET BACK MY HAIR.

I KNOW THAT IT'S A FACT OF LIFE
THAT EV'RYBODY DIES SOMEDAY.
BUT I'VE HAD MY SHARE OF GRIEF AND STRIFE.
AND I'VE GOT TOO MANY GAMES TO PLAY.

I DON'T CARE HOW
OR WHAT IT TAKES.
FOR ONCE AND ALL I'M ELIMINATING SICKNESS.
I'LL PURGE THIS POX
HAVE RADIANT LOCKS
OF BOLD AND LAVISH LUXURIOUS THICKNESS.
YOU'LL SEE HOW STRONG I'VE GROWN.
I'LL DO THIS ON MY OWN.
INTO THE FACE OF DEATH I'LL STARE.
I'LL STARE HIM DOWN AND TAKE BACK MY HAIR.

DANI. *(cont.)*
    YES EVERYONE DIES.
    AND LIFE IS UNFAIR.
    BUT THAT'S ALL LIES,
    CAUSE I'M WELL AWARE
    THAT A GIRL CANNOT DIE
    NO, A GIRL WILL NOT DIE WHO HAS
    FRENCH TWISTED, PONYTAILED, BRAIDED AND DYED,
    PERMED, AND CONDITIONED, AND MOOSED, AND BLOW
       DRIED,
    TEASED, AND GELLED, AND PULLED IN A BUN,
    COIFFURED, AND SPRAYED, AND RIBBONED, UPDONE,
    HEALTHY AND BEAUTIFUL,
    INVINCIBLE,
    UNBEATABLE
    HAIR!

MOTHER. And forever shall be, Amen. There. Now how are you feeling?

DANI. Better.

MOTHER. See? Shall I fluff Madame's pillows before her nap?

DANI. No, I have to get to work.

MOTHER. Work?

DANI. *(innocently)* Sleep.

MOTHER. Danica, this isn't a game. You need all of your energy to beat it. You keep getting all wound up with your little adventures, you'll wind up with pneumonia on top of it all.

DANI. Aw, Mom –

MOTHER. You need rest. No more playing.

DANI. But –

MOTHER. I don't want to hear another word about it. To bed. I have to have a chat with whoever's on duty. They're trying to move a new patient in here after I specifically told them you need a private room. I'll be back.

(She kisses **DANI** *on the head and exits.* **DANI** *bolts up out of her bed.)*

DANI. Why is cancer? A question no doubt best pursued through rigorous academic study.

(Enter **RAPH** *as* **TOMMY** *the schoolboy.)*

[MUSIC NO. 04A: **SCHOOL SEQUENCE**]

Good morning, class. Good morning, Master Fritz. Oh how thoughtful of you, Master Fritz, what a luminous candy apple. You are truly an exemplary scholar.

TOMMY. Good morning, Miss Lyons.

DANI. Oh. Thank you, Tommy. What a lovely gourd.

(music out)

(beat) As you no doubt recall, our topic for this week is acute lymphoblastic leukemia. Now then, class, can anyone recall some of leukemia's more common symptoms?

TOMMY. Miss Lyons. Could leukemia cause mild hallucinatory fantasies?

DANI. No Tommy, that is a very stupid question.

TOMMY. I was under the impression that there were no stupid questions.

DANI. That is a myth propagated to appease stupid people. Yes, Master Fritz? *(pause)*

[RESUME MUSIC NO. 04A: **SCHOOL SEQUENCE**]

Excellent, Master Fritz. That is an exhaustive list of leukemia's symptoms. Now, a patient can be diagnosed with A.L.L. before she is even one year old, and battle it until she is six. And tell me this: How do other children treat the child?

TOMMY. With respect, and reverence, and compassion.

DANI. No. The evil normal children are not sympathetic. They point, and stare, and use rude names which reveal their ignorance. And, even if she beats the cancer once, it does not necessarily mean –

*(enter **MARTY**, with a superhero suitcase)*

DANI. *(cont.)* What's this?

*(**RAPH** shrugs.)*

A new student in our class? And what is your name, young man?

*(**MARTY** sits on his bed.)*

Well, isn't that interesting, class? *(pause)* is a very interesting name. And, tell me, *(pause)* what school did you attend before transferring to prestigious PedOnc Prep?

(He turns on the TV.)

You know what? Boys are stupid!

*(**MARTY** turns up the volume.)*

You know what else? Star Trek is stupid!

(He shoots her a look.)

Come, class, pencils out. It is time for our test. Ready? Based on all that we have learned, write an essay in response to the following prompt: Why is cancer? Ready. Go.

(pause)

Go.

(pause)

Go!

*(**TOMMY** runs out.)*

What's wrong? Doesn't anyone have an answer? Not even you, Master Fritz?

*(to **MARTY**)*

What about you, do you know why cancer is?

*(**MARTY** turns up the TV)*

You're right, Master Fritz, if he cannot complete the essay we shall simply have to give him failing marks on his report card.

(She takes his chart from the foot of his bed.)

DANI. *(cont.)* Hm. This is curious, Master Fritz. This isn't the report card for a student named *(pause)* at all. It's the medical chart for a patient named –

MARTY. Marty.

DANI. Merriweather.

MARTY. My name is Marty.

DANI. But that can't be right. Merriweather sounds like a girl's name.

MARTY. It's Marty I tell you.

DANI. Merriweather Flowers.

MARTY. Marty Luke McFly Skywalker.

DANI. It also says here that Merriweather is a big weenie.

MARTY. It does not.

DANI. Oh no. I was mistaken. It says super big weenie.

MARTY. Give me that!

(He lunges for it. She runs away. He gives chase.)

DANI. Nyah-nyah. Nyah-nyah-nyah.

MARTY. Give it to me.

DANI. Make me!

MARTY. Hand it over or I will blast you with my proton pack.

DANI. What's a proton pack?

MARTY. A nuclear accelerator invented by Dr. Egon Spengler which emits a positively charged atomic beam that attracts negatively charged endoplasmic entities allowing for greater ease in their capture.

DANI. You don't have one of those.

MARTY. Do too.

DANI. Prove it.

MARTY. I do not have to prove anything to the likes of you.

DANI. I knew you didn't have one. Too bad. If you did, we could use it to kidnap one of these so-called doctors and interrogate him as to the reasons for cancer. As it is, I shall simply have to learn the secret by becoming a doctor myself.

MARTY. What?

DANI. Yes, as a doctor, I'll be able to discover everything.

MARTY. That is the dumbest idea I have ever heard.

DANI. All I need is a patient with cancer to operate on.

MARTY. Don't even think about it.

DANI. Come on, if you don't play how am I supposed to… what's that, Mr. Fritz? *(pause)*

*[MUSIC NO. 05: **DOCTOR SEQUENCE**]*

No, Mr. Fritz, I couldn't allow you to. It's too dangerous. *(pause)* Yes, I know it's in the name of science, but you could…I could lose you. *(pause)* You're a very brave bear, Mr. Fritz. And the best friend a girl could ask for. Thank you.

*(Enter **RAPH** as **J.D.** the surgeon. Music Cue: begin measure 5 of **DOCTOR SEQUENCE**.)*

DOCTOR.

J.D.

DOCTOR.

DANI.

DOCTOR.

J.D.

DOCTOR.

DANI. Today, doctor, we will be performing an arthroscopic anterior postpartum biopsy.

J.D.

HAS THE SUBJECT BEEN ANESTHETIZED, DOCTOR?

DANI. The subject, doctor, is named Mr. Fritz. You will treat him as a human being, and not as a mere number as is this hospital's usual wont. Are we clear?

J.D.

YES, DOCTOR.

DANI. Excellent.

>SCALPEL.

J.D.

>SCALPEL.

DANI.

>CLAMP.

J.D.

>CLAMP.

DANI.

>BUBBLE GUM.

J.D.

>BUBBLE GUM.

DANI.

>DAMMIT, DOCTOR. I TOLD YOU NO BIG LEAGUE CHEW.

J.D. I'm sorry, doctor.

DANI. I'm opening him up. Careful, doctor. We must not touch the sides or his nose will flash bright red and it will be most embarrassing on our parts. *(she cuts him open)* Interesting.

J.D.

>WHAT IS IT, DOCTOR?

DANI.

>STUFFING, DOCTOR, STUFFING.

J.D. Doctor, could stuffing be the cause of cancer?

DANI. Don't be ridiculous, doctor.

RAPH. BEEP.

DANI. What was that?

RAPH. BEEP-BEEP.

DANI. Oh no.

J.D. BLOOD PRESSURE DROPPING.

DANI. I need forty cc's of Mountain Dew, stat.

RAPH. BEEP-BEEP-BEEP.

J.D. He's flatlining!

DANI. Hang on, Mr. Fritz. Hang on.

J.D. We're losing him.

DANI. Not on my watch.

RAPH. BEEEEEEEEEEEEEEEEEEEE –

DANI. Clear!

 (She charges the defibrillator and zaps Mr. Fritz.)

RAPH. BEEP…BEEP.

DANI. Hold on, buddy.

J.D. BLOOD PRESSURE RISING.

DANI. Oh, thank God.

 MR. FRITZ, I THOUGHT I'D LOST YOU. MR. FRITZ?
 Mr. Fritz? Speak to me. What's wrong?

 (music out)

J.D. I'm no brain surgeon, doctor, but I'd say he's in a coma.

DANI. No. Mr. Fritz.

RAPH. Face it, kid. He's dying.

DANI. Shut up, Raph.

RAPH. Don't shoot the messenger.

DANI. Just…get lost.

 (He exits. **MARTY** *approaches* **DANI.***)*

MARTY. I'm sorry about your bear.

DANI. It's okay.

MARTY. I'm dying too, you know.

DANI. What do you mean?

MARTY. I vomited nine times last night.

DANI. So?

MARTY. It was orange.

DANI. So?

MARTY. So? That's how I know I'm dying.

 (she looks at him)

DANI. Big deal. One night I threw up ten times. And it was green with little purple chunks.

MARTY. I was lying. I really vomited eleven times.

DANI. I threw up twenty six times one night.

MARTY. You did?

DANI. Yep.

MARTY. Oh.

DANI. Look, what kind of cancer do you have anyways?

MARTY. Hodgkin's.

DANI. Oh, please. Hodgkin's is a sissy cancer. Mr. Fritz has ovarian cancer and he's not dying. I'm going to find out why cancer is and then everything will be back to normal.

MARTY. What are you talking about?

DANI. Once I figure out why it is I'll get my hair back.

MARTY. That doesn't make sense.

DANI. But it's true.

MARTY. That's stupid.

DANI. You're just jealous because I'm going to get my hair back and you'll still be looking all Captain Kirk.

MARTY. It's Picard.

DANI. What?

MARTY. Picard is bald. Captain Kirk has a bountiful head of hair.

DANI. So, do you want to play?

MARTY. No.

DANI. It's perfectly safe. I promise.

MARTY. Do you pinky swear?

(She sighs.)

DANI. Fine.

(She extends her pinky.)

MARTY. Of course you know that the pinky swear is childhood's most sacred bond, and if you break it, the pinkie monster will eat your soul.

(She lowers her pinky.)

In that case…

(He turns the TV back on.)

DANI. So, you're just going to sit there?

MARTY. Nope. There's an Indiana Jones marathon.

DANI. Why do you like all those stupid movies anyways?

MARTY. Stupid movies? Stupid movies? Please. They are not stupid. They are far from stupid. They are…they are…

*[MUSIC NO. 06: **WHY I LOVE THE MOVIES**]*

WHEN THE PREVIEWS END,
AND THE CREDITS START,
I FEEL A THUMPING
IN MY HEART.

I FORGET I'M ME,
FOR IT'S THEN I SEE
A WHOLE NEW REALITY.

INDIANA TRACKS ANCIENT ARTIFACTS.
ARKS, AND GRAILS, AND WEIRD PAGAN STONES.
HE IS A LOST ARK RAIDER, AND HE'S THE LAST CRUSADER.
YOU DO NOT MESS WITH DOCTA' JONES.

HE IS A MASTER OF ARCHAEOLOGY.
HONESTLY, WHAT'S NOT TO LIKE
ABOUT A MAN WHO'S THE SPAWN OF SEAN CONNERY?
AND WHO FIGHTS THE THIRD REICH?

CAUSE A HERO MAY NOT GET ALL THE BREAKS.
AND A HERO MAY BE AFRAID OF SNAKES.
BUT IT'S WISECRACKS THAT A HERO MAKES.
AND THAT'S WHY I LOVE THE MOVIES.

CLARK KENT, THAT MAN IS SURE HELL BENT
ON FOILING LEX LUTHER'S FUN.
HE'LL STOP THE VILLAIN'S PLAN, BECAUSE HE'S SUPERMAN.
POWERED BY RAYS FROM THE SUN.

IMAGINE HOW IT MUST FEEL
TO BE THE MIGHTY MAN OF STEEL.
STRONG AS A FREIGHT TRAIN,
IMPERVIOUS TO PAIN.

MARTY.

> YES? A HERO MIGHT FACE KRYPTONITE.
> AND A HERO MAY LOSE HIS SUPER SIGHT.
> BUT NO WEAKNESS WILL STOP A HERO'S FIGHT.
> AND THAT'S WHY I LOVE THE MOVIES.
>
> A HERO ALWAYS SAVES THE DAY.
> A HERO NEVER RUNS AWAY.
> A HERO ALWAYS TAKES A STAND.
> A HERO GETS THE LADY'S HAND.
>
> *(He reaches out, lost in the fantasy, and grabs* **DANI***'s hand. Then catches himself.)*
>
> BUT THAT'S TOTALLY GROSS. AND GRATUITOUS. AND
>   SUPERFLUOUS.
> THAT'S NOT WHY I LOVE THE MOVIES.
>
> I LOVE HOW A HERO FLIES,
> SOARING HIGH THROUGH THE NIGHTTIME SKIES.
> YOU NEVER HEAR A HERO CRY.
> YOU NEVER SEE A HERO DIE.
>
> YES A HERO MAY FEEL THE ENEMY NEAR.
> BUT A HERO WILL NOT SHED A TEAR.
> NO, A HERO WILL NOT LIVE IN FEAR.
> AND THAT'S WHY I LOVE –
> AND THAT'S WHY I LOVE –
> AND THAT'S WHY I LOVE THE MOVIES.

DANI. Well, you want a little adventure? Here's your chance.

MARTY. What?

> *(Enter* **RAPH,** *as* **PROFESSOR VON FATTENSCHTUFF,** *the scientist.)*

FATTENSCHTUFF. It vould seem zat ze tumors uf teddy bears are too schmall to examine mit ze naked eye. Ergo, ve have developed un procedure vich vill allow for a more thorough scientific investigation uf ze causes uf cancer.

MARTY. Who is that?

DANI. You can see him? *(to* **RAPH***)* He can see you?

FATTENSCHTUFF. Zis miniaturization ray vill miniaturize you to a nearly subatomic level. You vill then be inserted into ze bear, vich vill allow you to interrogate ze tumor in order to underschtand its root cause.

MARTY. What is he talking about?

FATTENSCHTUFF. However, ze effects uf ze ray vill only last for approximately six minutes und thirty seven seconds, so you must quickly vacate ze body or you vill be essentially, how you say, crushed. Any qvuestions?

MARTY. Yes –

FATTENSCHTUFF. Nein? Zen good luck.

(He aims the gun.)

MARTY. Hey –

(He shoots and exits.)

*[MUSIC NO. 06A: **IN THE BODY**]*

What the heck was that all about?

DANI. Whoa. Where are we?

MARTY. The hospital.

DANI. No, look.

MARTY. I don't see –

(She covers his eyes.)

DANI. No…look.

(She uncovers his eyes.)

MARTY. What in the name of Jupiter?

DANI. We must be inside of Mr. Fritz.

MARTY. Oh, sugar. I'll miss *Temple of Doom.*

DANI. Don't be such a wuss.

MARTY. I'm not a wuss.

DANI. This must be the stomach.

MARTY. And…what is our final destination?

DANI. Duh. The ovary.

MARTY. Oh. Right. And where exactly is that?

DANI. Jeez. You really don't know anything about human anatomy, do you? We have to go through the small intestine to the appendix, and then into the bloodstream, which will carry us to the testes, and finally to the ovary.

MARTY. I knew that.

DANI. C'mon.

 (**DANI** *leads* **MARTY** *to the bloodstream.*)

There's the bloodstream. Follow me.

(They swim through the bloodstream.)

MARTY. This is disgusting.

DANI. Stop being such a wimp. It's fun.

MARTY. Is it just me, or does the blood seem to be getting somewhat more rapid in pace?

DANI. Look, up ahead: the fallopian tubes.

MARTY. Oh dear. They look awfully steep.

DANI. Here we go!

 (They slide down the tubes.)

DANI. Wheeeeeeeeee!   **MARTY.** Ahhhhhhhhhhh!

MARTY. That was the single most horrifying experience of my life.

DANI. Oh, you loved it.

MARTY. Did not.

DANI. Look. The ovary!

 (enter **CANCER***)*

Oh no.

MARTY. What? It's just your weird friend guy.

DANI. No. It's Cancer.

MARTY. That's cancer?

DANI. Excuse me, Mr. Cancer?

CANCER. Well look at what we got here.

DANI. We were wondering if we might have a moment of your time.

CANCER. I did plan on spending the day eating this teddy bear from the inside out. But, you don't see a lot of company in a stuffed animal's ovary.

DANI. Sir, could you tell us why you are?

CANCER. Oh, that's a good one. No one's asked me that before. Of course, no one's asked me much of anything before. I don't get out much. I am Cancer.

DANI. I see.

CANCER. Why I'm here, huh? That's simple. The bear deserves me.

DANI. What?

CANCER. This bear did something wrong, and so here I am.

DANI. That's not true.

MARTY. Dani, maybe we should get going.

CANCER. It's his own damn fault.

MARTY. Dani –

DANI. You take that back.

CANCER. The bear deserves me, and so do you.

DANI. Liar!

    (**DANI** *charges* **CANCER**)

    Hi-ya!

    (**CANCER** *laughs.*)

CANCER. You're gettin' worse, girlie.

    (*With a wave of his hand he knocks them back into the bloodstream.* **DANI** *coughs. The lights go back to reality for a moment. Enter* **MOTHER.**)

MOTHER. Shh. You're alright.

DANI. It hurts.

MOTHER. Your A.N.C. is down. But we've seen worse.

CANCER. Worse.

DANI. I don't feel good.

MOTHER. It's just the methotrexate.

CANCER. And worse.

DANI. It hurts.

CANCER. And worse!

(DANI *coughs.*)

MOTHER. I'll get a nurse.

(*She exits.*)

MARTY. Dani! Help!

(*The lights return to fantasy.*)

DANI. We're being flushed into the bloodstream. He's trying to keep us in the body until the effects of the ray wear off.

MARTY. Get us out of here.

CANCER. Oh, and one more thing.

(*He throws a pillow, which attaches itself to* MARTY*'s face.*)

DANI. Merriweather!

MARTY. (*through pillow*) Mmm mmm iz mmm-mm.

DANI. What?

(*He removes the pillow briefly.*)

MARTY. I said, my name is – oh, forget it.

(*The pillow attacks him again.*)

DANI. It's a white blood cell. It must think we're some type of infection. Hang on.

MARTY. Mm!

(DANI *struggles with the pillow.*)

DANI. There's something vaguely ironic about this.

(*She removes the pillow.*)

MARTY. We're running out of time.

DANI. Quick, swim for the sphincter.

(They swim for the sphincter, and emerge just as they are restored to normal size. They collapse onto their beds.)

MARTY. You saved my life.

DANI. Don't mention it.

MARTY. And you quipped.

*[MUSIC NO. 07: **NO BIG DEAL**]*

DANI. I what?

MARTY. You quipped. You made wisecracks whilst saving me.

DANI. It was no big deal.

MARTY.

 I SUPPOSE.
 I MEAN, I'M SURE.
 IT'S JUST THAT
 NOBODY'S EVER DONE THAT FOR ME BEFORE.
 AND THAT'S WHY I FEEL
 THAT IT'S A KINDA BIG DEAL.

DANI.

 BUT IT'S NOT.
 IT'S QUITE OKAY.
 I DO IT FOR MR. FRITZ
 EIGHT TIMES A DAY.
 AND THAT'S WHY I FEEL,
 IT'S REALLY NOT A BIG DEAL.

MARTY.

 BUT IT IS A BIG DEAL.
 YOU KNOW, TO ME.
 IT'S A VERY BIG DEAL,
 CAUSE NOW I SEE
 THAT SOMETIMES HEROES ARE REAL.
 AND THAT'S A VERY BIG DEAL.

DANI.

 I'M TELLING YOU
 IT'S REALLY NOT.
 IT'S NOT A BIG DEAL
 TO SAVE A FRIEND YOU'VE FINALLY GOT.

AT LEAST ONE THAT'S REAL.

THAT'S REALLY NOT A BIG DEAL.

MARTY. I guess. Dani?

DANI. Yeah?

MARTY. Do you think this getting your hair back thing would work for me too?

DANI. Probably.

MARTY. Oh. Cause I think I know why cancer is.

DANI. You do?

MARTY. I think that tumor guy was right. You must've done something to deserve it.

DANI. That's ridiculous.

MARTY. No, I'm pretty sure it's true.

DANI. Merriweather, there is no evidence to suggest –

MARTY. Yuh-huh. Cause I broke the Gandalf the Gray bishop in my father's collector's edition Lord of the Rings chess set and then I had to come into the hospital.

DANI. Oh.

MARTY. So?

DANI. What?

MARTY. What did you do?

DANI. I don't know.

MARTY. Think.

DANI. I'm fairly certain I'm perfect.

MARTY. Oh. Well. Goodnight, then.

DANI. 'Night.

> (*They sleep.* **DANI** *dreams. Enter* **FATHER** *and* **MOTHER** *with the baby, in dream mode.*)
>
> *[MUSIC NO. 08: **DREAM SEQUENCE 2**]*

FATHER. Once upon…

MOTHER.   Once upon…

BOTH. Once upon a time.

FATHER. In the Kingdom of Blue Skies.

MOTHER. There lived a noble king.

FATHER. And a compassionate queen.

MOTHER. And as the sun rose high over their castle…

FATHER. They were blessed with a fearless…

MOTHER. A beautiful…

FATHER. A perfect –

(He turns away.)

MOTHER. My liege?

FATHER. My Queen, I must leave you.

MOTHER. What? What are you talking about, Will?

FATHER. And the princess.

MOTHER. You cannot do this to us.

FATHER. I must.

MOTHER. You son of a bitch.

FATHER. Tell her I went on a long journey, to a land far away.

MOTHER. And when she's old enough to ask why?

FATHER. M'lady, surely by then she will know the truth. What other reason could there be?

*(**FATHER** and the baby disappear. **DANI** approaches **MOTHER**, still in the dream.)*

DANI. Mom? What did he say?

(no response)

Tell me the end of the story.

MOTHER.
    NO MORE FAIRYTALE ENDINGS.
    NO MORE ONCE UPON A TIME.
    FANTASY NOW IS FORBIDDEN,
    AND STORIES A CRIME.

DANI. I need to hear the ending.

MOTHER.
    LET THE END GO UNSPOKEN.
    LET EACH TALE GO UNTOLD.
    AND LET THE QUEEN WHO ONCE LOVED THEM

GROW CALLOUS AND COLD.

IT'S CLEAR TO ME NO ONE ELSE SEES IT,
THE PRICE OF YOUR PERFECT BLUE SKIES.
THE WICKED WITCH QUEEN NOW DECREES IT,
THE END OF ALL FAIRYTALE LIES.

(She cackles. **DANI** *wakes with a start.)*

(music out)

DANI. Mom?!

MOTHER. Shh. You're alright. I'm here now.

DANI. Where's Daddy?

MOTHER. What? Dani, you were dreaming again. It's just you and me.

DANI. Oh. *(beat)* Why did Daddy leave?

MOTHER. That is a long story.

DANI. You can tell me.

MOTHER. Come on, get dressed.

DANI. What for?

MOTHER. You have your bone marrow aspirate. You know that.

DANI. No.

MOTHER. Don't start with me.

DANI. I don't want to.

MOTHER. Do you want to beat this?

DANI. I don't know if I can.

MOTHER. Don't talk that way. Look at me. Do you want to beat this?

DANI. Yes.

MOTHER. Then you don't have a choice. We need to know if the chemo is working.

DANI. I need to know why cancer is.

MOTHER. What?

DANI. I need to know why cancer is.

MOTHER. Oh, honey.

DANI. I went inside Mr. Fritz to find out –

MOTHER. What did I tell you about this?

DANI. But I couldn't figure out why it is.

MOTHER. That's because only God knows that.

DANI. Can we ask him?

MOTHER. Of course we can. We can pray.

DANI. Maybe you have to do something more drastic to get God's attention these days. I think I'll go to heaven and see him.

MOTHER. Not for a very long time.

DANI. No, I think I'll go now.

MOTHER. You will not. I will not lose you. *(beat)* Now come on, pray for our miracle.

DANI. I thought you said I already was a miracle.

MOTHER. You are, sweetheart, you are.

DANI. Mother? What if you only get one?

(beat)

MOTHER. The day you were diagnosed was the darkest day of my life. Your father pretended nothing was wrong, but I sat up all night staring out the window into this giant blackness. And I...I doubted. But when the sun rose that morning...I felt a hand on my shoulder, and I turned around and there in your crib your eyes lit up with the sunrise. And I saw God. And I promised him that as long as I could see the sunrise in those eyes...I would never doubt again.

(beat)

The minute we lose our faith, we lose our hope.

(beat)

Now get dressed. The nurses will be here any second.

DANI. I need my medallion.

MOTHER. You don't have it on?

DANI. I must have left it at the nurses' station. Or maybe outside somewhere.

MOTHER. You're washed and dressed when I get back.

(**MOTHER** *exits.*)

MARTY. Your mom's kind of mean, huh?

DANI. No she isn't. She's just…she isn't, okay?

MARTY. Okay.

DANI. C'mon. We've got to go.

MARTY. Where?

DANI. Heaven.

MARTY. I beg your pardon.

DANI. We have to go to heaven to find out why cancer is.

MARTY. I'm telling you, you must've done something –

DANI. That's not it. God's the only one who knows, so we have to ask him.

(*enter* **RAPH**)

RAPH. Not a chance.

DANI. It's the only way to get the answer.

RAPH. It's too dangerous.

DANI. You're just jealous because you didn't think of it first.

RAPH. It'll never work.

DANI. Will too.

RAPH. Will not.

DANI. Will too.

RAPH. Will not.

DANI. Will too.

RAPH. Do you have any idea how to get to heaven?

DANI. Rats.

MARTY. Do you have a thermonuclear hyperdrive?

DANI. A what?

MARTY. A thermonuclear hyperdrive. It's what makes space travel possible.

RAPH. Who is this kid?

MARTY. All you need is a thermonuclear hyperdrive, a craft capable of warp speed, and a cool fusion reactor and you can build a space ship.

DANI. And you'd do that for me?

MARTY. Sure.

DANI. Well then, what are we waiting for?

MARTY. Alright.

(He begins to build a space ship.)

RAPH. Mark my words, this is a bad idea.

MARTY. Your imaginary friend is somewhat pessimistic, isn't he?

DANI. Raph? He's not imaginary. He's my guardian angel.

MARTY. Oh. What's a guardian angel?

DANI. You know, one of God's angels who makes sure no bad things happen to you.

MARTY. Bad things like leukemia?

RAPH. I heard that.

DANI. That's something of a sore spot with Raph. He's not so great at protecting from chronic disease.

MARTY. Oh.

DANI. But he's real good at playing and stuff.

MARTY. I see.

DANI. Where's your guardian angel?

MARTY. My parents are atheists.

DANI. Oh. Would you like one?

MARTY. Really?

DANI. Sure. You can share Raph.

RAPH. I beg your pardon.

DANI. Hush up, you.

RAPH. Danica, the last thing I need is another –

DANI. Boy, I sure would hate to have to let God know that one of his guardian angels has difficulty following simple instructions, wouldn't you Merriweather?

RAPH. You fight dirty, kid.

DANI. So, you'll do it?

RAPH. I won't like it.

(he storms out)

MARTY. Excellent. Almost done.

DANI. Quick. Mother will be back any minute.

MARTY. I'm going as fast as I can.

DANI. Well go faster, Merriweather.

 (**MARTY** *waves his hand a la Obi Wan Kenobi.*)

MARTY. The boy's name is not Merriweather.

DANI. The boy's name is not Merriweather.

 (**MARTY** *looks at his hand in shock.*)

MARTY. *(hand again)* You will not call him Merriweather any more.

DANI. I will not call him Merriweather any more.

MARTY. *(hand thing)* You will call him…Marty.

DANI. I will call him…Merriweather. Ha!

MARTY. Oh, hell.

DANI. So…

MARTY. So…what coordinates shall I set?

DANI. Up?

MARTY. Do you have any idea how many star systems there are up there?

DANI. I don't know.

MARTY. How do you get to heaven?

DANI. Lead a good life?

MARTY. Are you serious?

DANI. If only we had a recently departed soul of someone kind and loving and selfless that we could follow there…

MARTY. But who do we know that's dying?

 (*Special on Mr. Fritz. They both look.*)

 [*MUSIC NO. 09:* ***REQUIEM FOR A BEAR***]

DANI. Oh.

MARTY. You don't have to –

DANI. No. I do.

 HIS FUR WAS TORN AND SCRATCHY,

IN PLACES WORN AND PATCHY.
HIS SEAMS WERE BARE,
BUT STILL I SWEAR
NOT ANYWHERE

DANI. *(cont.)*

A BETTER BEAR.
NOW LIFE SURE IS THE PITS.
REQUIEM FOR MR. FRITZ.

HE WAS THE PERFECT SIZE FOR HUGGING.
HE EXCELLED AT NIGHTTIME SNUGGLING.
HE TRULY CARED,
HE WAS ALWAYS THERE.
HE WAS TOUGH BUT FAIR,
THE BESTEST BEAR.
SOMETIMES A FRIEND JUST FITS.
REQUIEM FOR MR. FRITZ.

AND WHEN I DECIDED TO PAINT YOU GREEN,
OR STYLE YOUR FUR WITH VASELINE,
AND MOTHER PUT YOU THROUGH THE WASHING MACHINE,
YOU STILL CAME OUT ALL NICE AND CLEAN.

YOUR TINY BLACK FORGIVING EYES.
THAT BEG NOT TO MAKE THIS GOODBYE,
THEY SAY "HOLD ME THERE,
AND DON'T YOU DARE
DOUBT OR DESPAIR."
BUT I JUST CAN'T BEAR…
MY HEART IS TORN TO BITS.
REQUIEM FOR MR. FRITZ.

AND SO I OFFER THIS PRAYER.
THE WORLD IS CRUEL,
THE WORLD IS UNFAIR.
BUT IF THERE IS A GOD ANYWHERE,
PLEASE BLESS MY POOR LITTLE BEAR.
REQUIEM, NOW PAIN SHALL CEASE.
REQUIEM, MR. FRITZ,
IN ETERNAL PEACE.

MARTY. I'm sorry, Dani.

DANI. He would have wanted it this way. Now, follow that
  bear!

MARTY. Yes, ma'am.

  (They board the ship.)

  *[MUSIC NO. 10: **GOING TO HEAVEN**]*

DANI.

  HERE WE GO,
  TO MAKE ALL OUR ANSWERS CLEAR.
  EVEN THOUGH
  WE MUST TRAVERSE THE STRATOSPHERE.

  THROUGH THE AIR
  AND BEYOND ALL THE CONSTELLATIONS.
  ONCE WE'RE THERE
  WE'LL RECEIVE ALL OUR REVELATIONS.

DANI. *(cont.)*

  AND UP PAST THE CLOUDS
  WE'LL ASSUAGE ALL OUR DOUBT.
  CAUSE WE'RE GOING TO HEAVEN
  TO FIND OUT.

MARTY.

  BUCKLE UP.
  LOCK IN AUXILIARY POWER.
  WE DON'T WANT
  TO WIND UP IN A METEOR SHOWER.

  CHART A COURSE.
  AND PACK UP ALL PROVISIONS WE'LL NEED.
  USE THE FORCE.
  AND PREPARE FOR HYPERSPEED.

  I'LL FLY LIKE RED FIVE,
  'TIL AT LAST WE ARRIVE.
  CAUSE WE'RE GOING TO HEAVEN
  TO SURVIVE.

DANI.

  CAUSE IN HEAVEN
  WE WON'T FEEL SICK OR TIRED.

MARTY.
AND ON THE WAY
WE'LL DESTROY THE EMPIRE.

DANI.
IN HEAVEN
DISEASE WON'T GET THE BEST OF ME.

MARTY.
IN HEAVEN
I'LL FULFILL MY DESTINY.

BOTH.
CAUSE WE'RE GOING TO HEAVEN TODAY.

BEYOND THE SKIES
LIES GOD'S INFINITE MIND,
WHICH WE'RE GOING TO HEAVEN
TO FIND.

DANI. Wow.

MARTY. I know.

DANI. Look at all the stars. Sometimes, when I look at them, I can't help but think about how insignificant I am.

MARTY. Sometimes, when I look at them, I can't help but think about E.T.

(An alarm sounds.)

DANI. What the heck is that?

MARTY. We're getting some kind of gravitational pull from that small moon.

DANI. That's no moon. It's a giant tumor.

(The ship begins to shake.)

MARTY. We're caught in its tractor beam.

(They clutch each other and close their eyes.)

BOTH. Ahhhhhhhhhhhhhhhhhh!

(The ship stops shaking. They open their eyes.)

DANI. What happened?

MARTY. We must be inside the tumor.

DANI. How do we get out?

MARTY. We have to deactivate the tractor beam. I'll go.

DANI. I'll come with you.

MARTY. No. This is something I must do alone. If I'm not back in five minutes, leave without me.

DANI. Alright.

MARTY. You're supposed to at least protest a little bit.

(He begins to run off.)

DANI. Merriweather!

(He turns.)

MARTY. Ugh!

DANI. Good luck.

(He exits. Heavy breathing is heard.)

DANI. *(cont.)* Hello? Merriweather?

(enter **CANCER,** *as* **DARTH CANCER***)*

DARTH CANCER.
AND SO WE MEET AGAIN,
DANICAN.

DANI. Cancer.

DARTH CANCER. That's Darth Cancer to you.
THERE WILL BE
NO ESCAPE
THIS TIME.

DANI. I'll teach you to stand between a girl and her hair.

(She unleashes her light saber. He does the same. They fight.)

DARTH CANCER.
YOU'LL NEVER WIN FOOLISH CHILD.
DON'T YOU REALIZE I'M INSIDE?

DANI. That's not true.

DARTH CANCER. Give in to the power of the dark side.

DANI. No.

DARTH CANCER.
>YOU CAN'T DEFEAT ME INSOLENT YOUTH.
>SEARCH YOUR FEELINGS, IT'S THE TRUTH.
>IT'S THE TRUTH.

DANI. I'll never give in to you.

DARTH CANCER. Your mother never told you the truth about your father.

DANI. Please, I'm supposed to believe that you're my father? Cancer is my father?

DARTH CANCER. Not exactly. She never told you why he left.

DANI. He went on a long journey, to a land far, far away.

DARTH CANCER.
>THAT IS WHAT SHE'D HAVE YOU BELIEVE.
>BUT YOU KNOW FULL WELL JUST WHAT MADE HIM LEAVE.

DANI. What are you talking about?

DARTH CANCER.
>YOU KNOW WHY, YES YOU DO,
>YOUR FATHER LEFT BECAUSE OF YOU.

DANI. No!

DARTH CANCER.
>YOU KNOW IT'S TRUE.

DANI. NO!

DARTH CANCER.
>BECAUSE OF YOU!

(She charges passionately. **DARTH CANCER** *knocks her to the ground.)*

Now, feel the true power of the dark side.

(He stretches out his hand. She coughs violently. The lights flicker between fantasy and reality. **DANI** *is alone for a long moment.)*

(enter **MARTY***)*

MARTY.
>UNHAND HER, CANCER, AND PREPARE
>TO FIGHT A JEDI KNIGHT.

(**MARTY** *draws his twin lightsabers. They fight.*)

DARTH CANCER. Impressive, most impressive. But you're not a Jedi yet.

MARTY. You can't win, Cancer. If you strike me down I shall become more powerful than you could possibly imagine.

(*The fight continues.* **MARTY** *has* **DARTH CANCER** *on the retreat.*)

Hey, Darth. Force this.

(*He cuts off* **DARTH CANCER**'*s hands.*)

DARTH CANCER.
YOU HAVE NOT SEEN THE LAST OF ME,
I'LL BE BACK, WAIT AND SEE.

(**DARTH CANCER** *exits.*)

MARTY. Are you okay?

DANI. I think so.

(*He helps her to the ship.*)

MARTY. Quick. He won't be gone for long.

DANI. You saved my life.

MARTY. No, I just scared him off. He'll be back.

DANI. But…together, we'll be ready for him.

MARTY. Yeah, I guess we will.

DANI. And together, we can beat him.

MARTY. Yeah, I guess we can.

DANI. Thank you. Marty.

MARTY.
IT'S NO BIG DEAL.

DANI.
YES, IT'S STRANGE BUT IT'S TRUE:
BY MYSELF JUST WON'T DO.
SO I'M GOING TO HEAVEN
WITH YOU.

MARTY.
> NOW I KNOW I CAN DO
> WITHOUT HAN OR R2.
> CAUSE I'M GOING TO HEAVEN
> WITH –

BOTH.
> UP PAST FOREVER,
> WE'LL BE TWICE AS CLEVER.
> CAUSE WE'RE GOING TO HEAVEN
> TOGETHER.

DANI. Now, follow that bear!

(The ship blasts off. They fly through space.)

*[MUSIC NO. 10A: **GOING TO HEAVEN PLAY OFF**]*

MARTY. Captain's Log: Stardate, April 17th, 1991. The fearless Captain McFly Skywalker begins his venture into the most remote regions of the galaxy.

DANI. You keep a space diary?

MARTY. It's not a diary, it's a space journal.

DANI. Sounds a lot like a diary.

*(enter **MOTHER**)*

MOTHER. Sweetie?

(music out)

(The lights return to reality.)

What are you doing?

MARTY. Egad! Unidentified alien life form at nine o'clock.

DANI. Nothing.

MOTHER. You've got some color in your cheeks. Feeling any better?

DANI. Uh-huh.

MOTHER. They're saying a novena for you at Holy Trinity today.

DANI. Oh.

MOTHER. I thought maybe you'd feel up to going.

DANI. Oh. Can I just stay here instead?

(beat)

MOTHER. Sure.

DANI. You can still go though. If you want.

MOTHER. You'll be okay without me?

DANI. Marty will be here.

MARTY. Transfer all power to the rear deflector shields!

MOTHER. Is that supposed to reassure me?

MARTY. Hey!

MOTHER. Colleen is on duty, if you need anything, and I mean anything-

DANI. Mother…

MOTHER. I'll only be an hour or two.

(She exits. The lights return to fantasy.)

[RESUME MUSIC NO. 10A: **GOING TO HEAVEN PLAY OFF**]

MARTY. Enemy craft eliminated. Preparing for landing in heaven.

(They land and disembark.)

DANI. Whoa, the pearly gates.

MARTY. Look a little fake, if you ask me.

DANI. Come on.

*(enter **CANCER,** as **ST. CANCER**)*

Excuse me.

*(**ST. CANCER** turns.)*

Cancer!

(music out)

ST. CANCER. Well, well, well.

MARTY. Not again.

ST. CANCER. Surprised? You shouldn't be. I'm quite ubiquitous.

DANI. Where's St. Peter?

ST. CANCER. He wasn't union. Perhaps there's something I can help you with.

DANI. I…that is…

MARTY. We'd like to see God.

ST. CANCER. Beg pardon?

MARTY. God. We would like to speak to him…her… whatever.

ST. CANCER. Oh dear. I'm afraid I have some very bad news for you children. Hasn't anyone told you?

DANI. Told us what?

ST. CANCER. God is dead.

> [MUSIC NO. 11: **GOD IS DEAD**]

MARTY. What?

DANI. You're lying.

ST. CANCER. He died in nineteen seventy three. Guess what got him.

DANI. I don't believe you.

ST. CANCER.
> GOD IS DEAD.
> HAD A TUMOR IN HIS HEAD.
> HE WAS LOOKING GRIM AND GHASTLY
> AS ST. PETER FILLED WITH DREAD.
> THE SERAPHIM WERE AWED
> BY A BALD AND BLOATED GOD.
> CAN'T YOU SEE THE BIG, BAD LORD
> STUCK IN HEAVEN'S CANCER WARD?
> JESUS PRAYED.
> AND MARY WAS DISMAYED.
> AS THEY WATCHED THE FATHER'S CANCER SLOWLY SPREAD.
> THE ALPHA AND OMEGA
> BECAME A BUBBLING BEGGA'.
> SPIRIT'S SPED.
> TEARS BE SHED.
> GOD IS DEAD.

DANI. That isn't true.

MARTY. Yeah.

ST. CANCER. I'm afraid so, kids.

> GOD IS GONE.
> THE OLD BOY DONE PASSED ON.
> ETERNAL DEITY
> IT WOULD SEEM WAS ONE BIG CON.
> HE WAS SURE SURPRISED
> WHEN I METASTASIZED.
> THE ANGELS ALL ARE SOBBING,
> BUT YOURS TRULY'S HEART IS THROBBING.
> I COULD SING.
> GOD'S A PRISSY, SISSY THING.
> HE CLAIMED TO BE A KING, BUT HE'S A PAWN.
> IT WOULD SEEM THE MIGHTY MAKER
> WAS JUST A FLIGHTY FAKER.
> HIS SWAN SONG.
> SAY SO LONG.
> GOD IS GONE.

DANI.

> YOU'RE THE ONE WHO'S DYING.
> YOU'RE A LIAR AND YOU'RE LYING.
> YOU'RE A FOOL AND YOU'RE FULL
> OF HOT AIR.

MARTY.

> MAYBE YOU COULD BEAT US WHEN WE'RE SEPARATE.
> BUT NOW WE ARE TOGETHER
> SO PREPARE.

DANI/MARTY.

> TOO LONG WE'VE JUST BEEN WHINING.
> SO OUR POWERS ARE COMBINING.
> AND TWO FORCES ARE MORE POWERFUL THAN ONE.

MARTY.

> WE'LL MAKE YOU TAKE IT BACK

DANI/MARTY.

> WHEN TOGETHER WE ATTACK!

> *(They attack.* **ST. CANCER** *knocks them to the ground and tortures them telepathically.)*

ST. CANCER.
> GOD IS THROUGH.
> THE BIG GUY CROAKED AND SO WILL YOU.
> YOU'RE SURE TO SUFFER SLOWLY
> NO MATTER WHAT YOU DO.

ST. CANCER. *(cont.)*
> TOGETHER, ONE BY ONE,
> MAKES NO DIFFERENCE YOU'RE BOTH DONE.
> YOU TWERPS WON'T EVER BEAT ME,
> TWO SICK KIDS CANNOT DEFEAT ME.
> DO YOU JEST? THAT'S YOUR BEST?
> YOU WILL SURELY FAIL THIS TEST.
> LET ME BID YOU BOTH A VERY FOND ADIEU.
> WHY WOULD I EVER LIE?
> YOU BOTH ARE DOOMED TO DIE.
> LET'S REVIEW.
> TAKE YOUR CUE.
> GET A CLUE.
> YOU KNOW IT'S TRUE.
> GOD IS THROUGH,
> AND SO ARE YOU!

> *(He laughs.)*

DANI. No!

MARTY. We're not giving up that easily.

ST. CANCER. Face it, kid, even together you don't stand a chance.

MARTY. Isn't there someone else we can talk to? What about that sandals guy?

DANI. Yeah, we'd like to speak with Jesus.

ST. CANCER. Jesus? Christ! I always forget about him.

DANI. Hah! We've got you.

ST. CANCER. Alright, you can see Jesus.

MARTY. Yes!

ST. CANCER. But first I'll need some documentation.

MARTY. What sort of documentation?

ST. CANCER. Just the basics, really. Proof of insurance, expired library card, and a C.O.D.

DANI. What's a C.O.D.?

ST. CANCER. Certificate of Death. They should have given you one on your way through Purgatory.

MARTY. There must be some mistake. We're not dead.

ST. CANCER. I beg your pardon.

DANI. We just wanted to ask one quick question.

ST. CANCER. Then, you're…still living?

MARTY. That is correct.

ST. CANCER. I see.

(He presses a button.)

Security.

DANI. What are you doing?

ST. CANCER. I'm afraid you can't get into heaven until you're dead.

MARTY. But –

ST. CANCER. Ta-ta.

DANI. But, you said we could see Jesus.

ST. CANCER. And you believed me? C'mon. I'm Cancer.

MARTY. That's not fair.

ST. CANCER. Come back when you're dead. Shouldn't be too long now.

[*MUSIC NO. 11A: **FALL FROM HEAVEN**]*

*(He presses another button. They fall from heaven and land in their beds. **DANI** begins coughing violently. She goes into a seizure. Enter **RAPH** as **FATHER** and **MOTHER** in dream mode)*

FATHER. Once upon…

MOTHER.   Once upon…

BOTH. Once upon a time…

FATHER. I must leave this place.

MOTHER. Do not do this. Please.

FATHER. I must.

MOTHER. Why?

FATHER. Because of her.

DANI. No!

(FATHER turns to DANI.)

FATHER. You wanted the ending, Princess. Once upon a time there lived a noble king and a compassionate queen.

DANI. Daddy, I –

FATHER. They lived happily in their blue sky kingdom. Until one day, along came a princess. Seemingly perfect. But the princess was cursed.

DANI. I don't want to –

FATHER. As the skies turned black, the princess began to change.

DANI. No.

FATHER. Before their eyes the beautiful baby transformed into a hideous, misshapen monster!

(DANI opens her mouth, but no sound comes out.)

The monster banished the king and left the queen a shadow of herself. No one lived happy ever after, because no matter how she tried, the princess could never, ever set things right!

(music out)

(DANI wakes with a start as FATHER leaves. She gasps for breath.)

DANI. Noooooooooooooo!

MOTHER. Shh. Shh. It's alright.

DANI. What's happening to me?

MOTHER. You had a seizure. But you're alright now, thank God. *(beat)* I never should have left you.

DANI. Where's Daddy?

MOTHER. Danica…he's gone.

DANI. When's he coming back?

MOTHER. I don't think he is.

DANI. Why not?

MOTHER. Not everyone is as brave and strong as you are.

DANI. I need one of his stories, a good story –

MOTHER. The last thing we need is one of his useless goddamn fairy tales. *(beat)* We need faith.

DANI. Mother? What if God is just another story?

(beat)

MOTHER. I have to let Dr. Michaels know you're awake.

(She exits.)

DANI. Marty! Psst. Marty!

(He wakes up.)

MARTY. What is it? Are you okay?

DANI. Yeah. *(beat)* No. I think I'm getting sicker.

MARTY. What are we going to do?

DANI. Jesus can give us the answer.

MARTY. But we can't get in to see him unless…

DANI. We have to die.

MARTY. Dani, no.

DANI. I don't mean really, I mean we have to play death, like a game.

MARTY. Death is not a game.

DANI. I need to set things right. Please, Marty, play.

MARTY. How do we do it?

DANI. Guns?

*(**MARTY** shakes his head.)*

Knives?

*[MUSIC NO. 11C: **LITTLE RAY'S ENTRANCE**]*

*(**MARTY** shakes his head. Enter **RAPH** as **LITTLE RAY**, the drug dealer. He slides under **MARTY**'s bed.)*

MARTY. What's going on?

LITTLE RAY. Sh, dawg! Be quiet for godsakes.

MARTY. Why?

LITTLE RAY. Why? Why? Isn't it obvious? I'm hiding out from the fuzz, man.

MARTY. What's the fuzz?

LITTLE RAY. C'mon, man. Don't you know anything? The fuzz, the pigs, the law, man, the cops.

MARTY. Oh.

DANI. I knew that.

LITTLE RAY. See man, I knew the little homegirl was down.

DANI. Why are you hiding from the police?

LITTLE RAY. Oh, man, don't you start with me too, man. Because I'm a drug dealer.

DANI. You are?

LITTLE RAY. Of course I am, man. See?

(He opens his coat.)

MARTY. And, are any of those narcotics available for purchase?

LITTLE RAY. Of course, bro.

*(MUSIC NO. 12: **LITTLE RAY'S RAP**)*

I GOT THE SMACK, THE HORSE, THE FROG, THE E.
THE X, THE Y, THE LMNOP.
I GOT THE CRACK, THE CRANK, THE CRUNK, THE SCOOBY
  DOO.
THE MARY JANE, THE MARY LOUISE, THE MARY SUE.
THE POT, THE PAN, THE PIB, THE PEZ, THE PEF.
THE KERMIT, THE FOZZY, THE PIGGY, AND THE SWEDISH
  CHEF.
THE BLIPPITY BLAPPITY SHAKALAKA BIP BAP BOP.
THE SNIP, THE SNOOP, THE SNAP, THE CRACKLEY POP.
THE REDS, THE ORANGE, THE PURPLE, THE YELLOWISH
  GREEN.
THE ZOOP, THE SHOOP, THE POOP, AND THE FRUITY LOOP.
WHATCHU KIDDOS NEED?

MARTY. Uh, might it be possible, my good sir, for one to overdose on any of said narcotics?

LITTLE RAY. Sure, dawg. I got…

    *[MUSIC NO. 12A: **LITTLE RAY'S RAP REPRISE**]*

    THE FRANK, THE BOMB, THE L, THE WACKAWACKA –

DANI. We were hoping, perhaps, for something a good deal…stronger.

LITTLE RAY. Oh, I see what you're saying. Damn, you kiddos don't mess around.

    (He pulls out a bottle.)

MARTY. Flinstones' Vitamins?

LITTLE RAY. Look closer, dawg.

MARTY. Flinstones' Vitamins…of Death.

DANI. Would you consider a couple of morphine drips fair trade?

LITTLE RAY. I like the way you think.

    (They make the exchange.)

RAPH. For what it's worth, we need to have a serious conversation about your exposure to inappropriate television content.

DANI. Raph.

RAPH. Kid, this is not the answer –

DANI. You're ruining it.

RAPH. There are things in this world that shouldn't be played with.

DANI. Go!

    *(He does. **MARTY** struggles with the bottle.)*

MARTY. It's childproof.

DANI. Here.

    (She opens it easily.)

MARTY. How many do you think it will take?

DANI. I dunno. I suppose a handful ought to do.

MARTY. That's what I was thinking.

DANI. You don't want to underdo these things.

MARTY. Right.

DANI. Okay. On the count of three.

> (*They each take a handfull of pills.*)

> One…two…

MARTY. Wait, waitwait! One, two, go on three, or one, two, three, go?

DANI. We go on three.

MARTY. Okay. Glad that's been cleared up.

DANI. Ready?

MARTY. Ready.

DANI. One…two…

MARTY. Dani?

DANI. Yeah?

MARTY. I'm not certain I want to play anymore.

DANI. Why not?

MARTY. I just don't wanna.

DANI. Come on.

MARTY. No.

DANI. What's the matter, McFly…chicken?

MARTY. No.

> (**DANI** *makes chicken noises.*)

> I'm not.

> (**DANI** *makes more chicken noises.*)

> Stop it!

> (**DANI** *makes even more chicken noises.*)

> Alright, fine! I'm scared.

DANI. Of what?

MARTY. Everything.

DANI. Aw, come on.

MARTY. No. You're right. I'm a lily liver, yellow belly, fraidy cat weenie. I'll always be scared.

DANI. Hey…

*[MUSIC NO. 13: **SIDE BY SUICIDE**]*

CHIN UP, NOW DON'T BE AFRAID.
IT'S JUST A GAME LIKE THE ONES WE'VE PLAYED.
AND YOU AND I HAVE GOT IT MADE.
JUST LOOK AT ME,
JUST LOOK AT ME.

I MAY NOT BE OLD AND I MAY NOT BE GROWN.
I MAY NOT KNOW MUCH, BUT I'VE ALWAYS KNOWN
THAT YOU WON'T BE SCARED IF YOU'RE NOT ALONE.
AND YOU GOT ME,
YES YOU GOT ME.

AND AS LONG AS WE'RE TOGETHER
THERE'S NO NEED TO FEAR WHATSOEVER.
CAUSE WE'LL BE STANDING THERE,
SIDE BY SIDE.

MARTY.

BUT WHAT IF IT'S NOT THE WAY WE THOUGHT?
WE MAY BE RIGHT, BUT WE MAY BE NOT.
AND I JUST CAN'T SHAKE ALL THESE FEARS I'VE GOT.
I'M SCARED YOU SEE.
I'M SCARED THAT WE

MIGHT GET THERE AND THEN WE LEARN
THAT THIS JESUS GUY IS SOMEWHAT STERN
AND ONCE YOU'RE THERE YOU CAN'T RETURN
SO EASILY.
SO EASILY.

DANI.

BUT AS LONG AS WE'RE TOGETHER,
THERE'S NO NEED TO FEAR WHATSOEVER.
CAUSE WE'LL BE STANDING THERE
SIDE BY SIDE.

MARTY.

BUT I'M AFRAID OF THE UNKNOWN.
ESPECIALLY IF I'M ALL ALONE.

DANI.

BUT IF I'M THERE YOUR FEARS WON'T LINGER.
IF YOU GET SCARED YOU CAN SQUEEZE MY FINGER.

    THEN ALL YOUR FEARS WILL RUN AWAY.
    AND FROM THEN ON I'LL ALWAYS STAY.

MARTY.

    BUT, HOW CAN I BE SURE THAT YOU'LL ALWAYS BE THERE?

DANI.

    I PROMISE.

MARTY.

    JUST PROMISE?

DANI.

    I PINKY SWEAR.

MARTY.

    WELL IN THAT CASE I SUPPOSE I'LL DARE.

DANI.

    YOU'LL STAY WITH ME?

MARTY.

    IF YOU STAY WITH ME.

DANI.

    PLEASE STAY WITH ME.

BOTH.

    THEN TAKE MY HAND AND HOLD IT TIGHT,
    AS WE GO GENTLE INTO THAT GOOD NIGHT.
    WE'LL WALK TOGETHER INTO THE LIGHT.
    DON'T YOU SEE?
    DON'T YOU SEE?

    THIS IS A BOND THAT NOTHING CAN BREAK.
    HAND IN HAND OUR HANDS WON'T SHAKE.
    NOT EVEN DEATH COULD EVER TAKE

DANI.

    YOU FROM ME.

MARTY.

    YOU FROM ME.

BOTH.

    YOU FROM ME.

    CAUSE AS LONG AS WE'RE TOGETHER,
    THERE'S NO NEED TO FEAR WHATSOEVER.

DANI.
> CAUSE NOW WE'RE STANDING SIDE –

MARTY.
> NOW WE'RE STANDING SIDE –

DANI.
> NOW WE'RE STANDING SIDE –

MARTY.
> NOW WE'RE STANDING –

BOTH.
> SIDE BY SIDE
> BY SUI-CIDE.

> *(She looks at him and takes his hand.)*

MARTY. Okay.

DANI. Here goes.

BOTH. One…two…

> *(They look at each other. Pause.)*

DANI. It is kind of scary, isn't it?

MARTY. Yeah.

DANI. Maybe…in the morning, it won't be so scary.

MARTY. Yeah. Good plan.

DANI. But, first thing tomorrow…

MARTY. Definitely. First thing.

DANI. Goodnight, Marty.

MARTY. Goodnight, Dani.

> *(pause)*
> Hey, Dani?

DANI. Yeah?

MARTY. Nothing.

> *(He goes to sleep. Enter **MOTHER**. She sits on **DANI**'s bed and touches her head.)*

DANI. Mother?

MOTHER. My beautiful, beautiful baby.

DANI. What's wrong? *(beat)* What did the doctor say?

MOTHER. Nothing.

DANI. Oh.

> *(beat)*

MOTHER. I wish your father were here.

DANI. I know why he left.

MOTHER. What?

DANI. It was because of me.

MOTHER. Oh, Dani, no.

DANI. It's all my fault.

MOTHER. Dani, listen to me. None of this is your fault. None of it.

DANI. But then, why?

MOTHER. Your father…he told beautiful stories. But a story is only as good as the truth inside it. And his stories… well, he was never very good with the truth. So, he ran.

DANI. Oh.

MOTHER. He was a coward, Dani.

DANI. Oh. *(beat)* I thought he was King William, the Lionheart.

MOTHER. There's only one Lionheart in this family.

DANI. Oh. *(beat)* No. I think there are two.

MOTHER. You should really get some –

DANI. I still miss his stories.

MOTHER. Say your prayers, angel. Please.

DANI. You know, maybe believing and make-believing aren't all that different.

MOTHER. What do you mean?

DANI. Well, maybe it's not so important how true something is. Maybe what really matters is how it makes you feel.

MOTHER. And, how did his stories make you feel?

DANI. Like no matter what, the ending would always be happy ever after.

MOTHER. Once upon a time…in the kingdom of blue skies. Lived a princess, fair and beautiful with magic in her eyes.

*[MUSIC NO. 14: **THE SUN STILL ROSE**]*

SHE WOULD DANCE WITH DANDELIONS,
AND WHISPER TO THE TREES.
AND THE KING AND QUEEN WOULD WATCH HER
AS SHE SET THEIR HEARTS AT EASE.

DANI. That's good, mommy.

MOTHER.

'TIL ONE DAY SHE FELL
UNDER A WICKED WITCH'S SPELL.
AND SHE LOST HER WAY ON THE FOOTPATH,
AS COLD, DARK NIGHTTIME FELL.

THE WOODS WERE BLACK.
SHE WAS AFRAID.
BUT THE SUN STILL ROSE THAT DAY.

AND BY DAWN'S FIRST LIGHT SHE DISCOVERED
THAT SHE WAS NEVER SO ALONE.
IN AN UNFAMILIAR FOREST,
SHE FELT TRULY ON HER OWN.

ALL THE CREATURES OF THE FOREST
HAD SOMEHOW DISAPPEARED.
AND IN THE SHADOWS OF HER SOLITUDE,
THE PRINCESS TRULY FEARED.

(**DANI** *pretends to sleep*)

AND THOUGH HER KING
HAD RUN AWAY,
THE SUN STILL ROSE THAT DAY.

THEN A FIRE BREATHING DRAGON
SWOOPED DOWN FROM THE SKIES.
WITH AN UNREMITTING ANGER,
NO PITY IN HIS EYES.

IN HIS UNFORGIVING CLAWS,
HE CAUGHT THE MAIDEN FAIR.
AND SWIFTLY HE IMPRISONED HER
IN HIS WRETCHED, LONELY LAIR.

THE CAVE WAS COLD,
AND FAR AWAY.
BUT THE SUN STILL ROSE THAT DAY.

MOTHER. *(cont.)*

> AND THE PAIN IT WAS UNBEARABLE,
> AND THE TEARS WELLED IN HER EYES.
> SO OFT BEFORE UNSCARABLE,
> THE PRINCESS BROKE DOWN AND CRIED.
>
> SHE TURNED HER FACE
> UP TO THE SKY.
> AND OUT LOUD THE PRINCESS ASKED THE HEAVENS "WHY?"
>
> AND AS DAWN BROKE,
> NO ANSWER CAME.
> BUT THE SUN STILL ROSE THAT DAY.
>
> AND THE QUEEN LOOKED ON HELPLESSLY,
> AS SHE WATCHED THE PRINCESS FADE.
> BUT THE BEAST INSIDE HER BABY
> SIMPLY WOULD NOT BE STAYED.
>
> ALL SHE COULD DO
> WAS KNEEL AND PRAY.
> SOMEHOW SHE KNEW
> NO OTHER WAY.
> INSTEAD OF BLUE
> THE SKY TURNED GREY.
> AS THE SUN STILL ROSE…
> THE SUN STILL ROSE…
> THE SUN STILL ROSE THAT DAY.
> THE SUN STILL… ROSE…

(She exits. **DANI** *sleeps. The lights come up on her the next morning.)*

DANI. Marty? Marty? Rise and shine, it's time to die.

(She notices his bed. It is empty and has been stripped.)

Marty?

(enter **RAPH** *)*

Where is he?

RAPH. He's gone.

DANI. Gone where?

RAPH. Kid…

(beat)

DANI. No.

RAPH. He left without you.

DANI. He wouldn't do that.

RAPH. He didn't have a choice.

DANI. He probably just went to the cafeteria.

RAPH. His suitcase is gone.

DANI. Or the rec room.

RAPH. His posters are gone.

DANI. Or to –

RAPH. His movies are gone.

(beat)

DANI. Well, maybe…maybe he had a miracle and was cured and –

RAPH. Kid.

*(He takes **MARTY**'s hat from the bedpost and tosses it to her.)*

He's gone.

DANI. No. Oh, Marty. *(beat)* I can't do this anymore, Raph.

RAPH. Alright.

DANI. I'm done.

RAPH. Okay. Here you go.

(He hands her the pill bottle.)

DANI. What is this, some kind of reverse psychology?

RAPH. No. Go on. Do it.

DANI. Last night you said –

RAPH. You convinced me.

DANI. Weird.

RAPH. Just do it.

(She throws the pills.)

DANI. No. I can't.

RAPH. Why not?

DANI. I can't do it alone.

RAPH. You're not –

DANI. Yes I am.

RAPH. Why don't we play a game?

DANI. No. That's what I'm talking about. No more stupid imagination.

RAPH. Well, that's too bad, because I've got a game that would knock your socks off.

DANI. Not interested.

RAPH. Your loss. It would make all of your pain go away. Forever.

*[MUSIC NO. 15: **COMALAND**]*

DANI. What is it?

RAPH.
> BLUE COTTON CANDY SKIES.
> FUNNEL CAKES, ICE CREAM CONES, CURLY FRIES.
> THE MUSIC OF CHILDREN'S MELODIC SQUEALS,
> GIGANTIC MAGICAL FERRIS WHEELS.
> IN COMALAND!

DANI. Comaland?

RAPH. Yeah, Comaland. It's like Disneyland. But not.
> COASTERS BEYOND COMPARE.
> TWIRLING AND SWIRLING YOU THROUGH THE AIR.
> A SWEET LITTLE PRINCESS CAN SEE SO CLEAR
> YOU CAN'T BE LONELY WHEN YOU ARE HERE.
> IN COMALAND, YOUR FEARS WILL HAVE FLOWN.
> IN COMALAND, YOU WON'T KNOW YOU'RE ALONE.
>
> AND IF YOU'VE LOST SOMEONE FOR WHOM YOU CARE,
> YOU WILL BE BLISSFULLY UNAWARE.
> IN COMALAND.

*(enter **MOTHER**)*

MOTHER. Danica?

DANI. Did you hear something?

RAPH. Nope.

DANI. I thought I heard –

RAPH.

SO IF YOU LOVE BEARS AND GAMES WITHOUT END,
STEP UP, TAKE A CHANCE, WIN A NEW STUFFED FRIEND.
IN COMALAND.

DANI.

IS IT TRUE THEY HAVE TEN THOUSAND RIDES?

RAPH.

NOT INCLUDING WATER SLIDES.

DANI.

MY VERY OWN MERRY GO ROUND?

RAPH.

HORSES THAT FLY OFF THE GROUND.
THINK WHAT THE PRICE OF ADMISSION'S WORTH
TO THE NUMBEST YET HAPPIEST PLACE ON EARTH.

MOTHER. Dani? Dani? Talk to me.

DANI.

ROLLER COASTERS RIP THROUGH THE NIGHT.
FEEL THE EXCITEMENT AND NOT THE FRIGHT.

RAPH.

RACE DOWN THE HILLS AND EMBRACE THE THRILLS.

DANI.

WILL I NEED NEEDLES, OR SHOTS, OR PILLS?

RAPH.

NOT IN COMALAND, YOU'LL FEEL HAPPY NOT SORE.
CAUSE IN COMALAND, YOU WON'T FEEL ANYMORE.

DANI. Okay. I'll play.

MOTHER. Open your eyes, sweetheart.

DANI. I could swear I heard my –

RAPH. Shut your goddamn mouth.

DANI. What did you say?

RAPH. *(mocking)* What did you say?

DANI. You're not Raph.

RAPH. No, really?

DANI. Cancer!

> (**RAPH** *becomes* **CANCER.**)

What have you done with Raph?

CANCER. What do you think?

DANI. You killed him? You killed Raph, you son of a –

> *(She tries to attack, but is restrained.)*

CANCER. You can't win now, stupid. You're in a coma.
> SO BUCKLE UP YOUR SAFETY BELT.

MOTHER. Oh God, Dani?

CANCER.
> PREPARE FOR A RIDE LIKE YOU'VE NEVER FELT.
> KEEP YOUR HANDS AND YOUR ARMS INSIDE.

MOTHER. Dani, look at me!

CANCER.
> SIT BACK, RELAX, AND ENJOY THE RIDE.

MOTHER. Doctor! Somebody, help!

CANCER.
> WHEN I THROW THIS LEVER
> YOU'RE STUCK HERE FOREVER.
> IN COMALAND.
>
> THE RIDE HAS BEGUN,
> THIS TIME CANCER HAS WON.
> FACE IT DANI, YOU'RE DONE.
> CAUSE IN COMALAND,
> YOU'LL BE HERE TILL YOU DIE!

> *(He throws the lever, laughs maniacally, and exits.)*
>
> *[MUSIC NO. 15A: **COMALAND TAG**]*

DANI. Wait! You can't…you can't…

> *(Voices swirl around her.)*

MOTHER.   Once upon a time…

CANCER.   You're in a coma…

MARTY.   I shall become more powerful than you could possibly imagine.

WINK. Why is cancer?

MOTHER. Only God knows, angel. Only God knows.

CANCER. God is dead.

MARTY. I'm dying too, you know.

DARTH CANCER. Search your feelings.

MOTHER. Sometimes the cancer is too much.

FATHER. I must go on a long and perilous journey…

MARTY. I think I'm getting worse.

CANCER. Worse and worse and worse.

MOTHER. Prayer always works.

WINK. Why is cancer?

MOTHER. Only God knows, angel. Only God knows.

CANCER. God is dead.

*[MUSIC NO. 15B: **GOD'S APPEARANCE**]*

(**DANI** *wakes up. A brilliant flash of light.* **GOD** *sits on her bed.*)

(music out)

DANI. Who are you?

GOD. That's a tough one. I go by a lot of names.

DANI. God?

GOD. That's one of them.

DANI. You look suspiciously similar to most of the adult males I've encountered in a dream-like state recently.

GOD. You see me as you need to see me.

DANI. Am I imagining this?

GOD. You can't. Your imagination shuts down when you're in a coma.

DANI. Really?

GOD. Go on and try.

(She does.)

DANI. I…I can't.

GOD. See?

DANI. Couldn't I be imagining that I can't imagine and therefore –

GOD. Sometimes, Dani, you just have to believe.

DANI. It's so…blah here.

GOD. True.

DANI. God? Why is cancer?

GOD. Wow.

DANI. I'm sorry, but it's urgent.

GOD. I don't have an answer for you, Dani.

DANI. You have to. You're –

GOD. What I know is this: Everything exists. Everything that could possibly be, is.

DANI. But –

GOD. Good and bad, courage and fear, joy and pain. They all are. Trouble is, they sometimes get all mixed up in the same wrapper. Like this.

(He produces a dandelion.)

DANI. A dandelion?

GOD. Most people call it a weed. To a flower, it is a thing of incredible danger. But, beneath the surface, it contains an intricate beauty.

(He transforms the dandelion into its "dead" state and blows the petals into the air.)

DANI. But, why?

GOD. That's the thing, Dani. Just because things are, doesn't mean they have a knowable reason.

DANI. They have to.

GOD. Why is love, Dani?

DANI. What?

GOD. Why is candy?

DANI. I –

GOD. Why is mint chocolate chip ice cream?

DANI. There's gotta be an answer.

GOD. I'm sorry, Dani.

DANI. Then…all the hospitals, and the treatments, everything…it's all for nothing.

GOD. Is it?

DANI. What?

GOD. Not having a reason doesn't make a thing worthless.

DANI. God?

GOD. Mm-hm?

DANI. I don't want to die.

GOD. I know. I know you don't. But death is another one of those things that just…is.

DANI. Isn't there something I can do? I'll do anything. Please.

GOD. I'm sorry. I really am.

DANI. But, you're God. Can't you just take the cancer out of my life completely?

GOD. Well, sure. I could.

DANI. You could?

GOD. Like it never happened. But, if I do, you'll lose everything that came with it.

DANI. I think I'd be okay with that.

GOD. Are you sure?

DANI. What do you mean?

GOD. Not everybody spends life living, Dani. You have.

DANI. Yeah, but not because of cancer.

GOD. What do you think sparked your incredible imagination?

DANI. Really? *(beat)* I'm through with all that.

GOD. What about this guy?

(*He produces Mr. Fritz.*)

DANI. Mr. Fritz!

GOD. Your mother gave him to you the day you were diagnosed.

DANI. Oh. You know, God, teddy bears are nice and all, but I don't think they're quite worth cancer.

GOD. Then I guess you're right. I guess it was all for nothing.

(enter **MARTY***)*

DANI. Marty?

MARTY. Hello, Dani.

DANI. You have hair.

MARTY. I know.

DANI. You got in?

MARTY. Uhm. Yes.

DANI. I thought the atheist thing might trip you up.

MARTY. Nope.

DANI. Oh.

MARTY. You'd really like it here.

DANI. What's it like?

MARTY. It's…the greatest thing you can possibly imagine.

DANI. I can't imagine. I'm in a coma.

MARTY. Oh.

(He puts his hands over her eyes.)

DANI. What are you –

(He removes them. She sees heaven.)

[RESUME MUSIC NO. 15B: ***GOD'S APPEARANCE]***

(music out)

Oh.

MARTY. I know.

DANI. Is there candy?

MARTY. It's all we eat.

DANI. And games?

MARTY. More than you could ever play.

DANI. And…and…

MARTY. Dani?

DANI. Yeah?

MARTY. There's nothing to be afraid of.

(He slowly backs away.)

GOD. I can give you life without cancer. It just won't be this one. It won't be yours. But, if that's what you want, I'll just go right ahead and –

DANI. Wait.

(She looks at **MOTHER**, *asleep in the chair.)*

[MUSIC NO. 16: *FINALE*]

Will I get to see my mom?

GOD. Any time you want.

DANI. I love you, mommy.

(She kisses **MOTHER** *on the forehead.* **MOTHER** *looks up, then touches the spot where* **DANI** *kissed her.)*

MOTHER. Dani? Oh my baby…

*(***GOD*** approaches* **MOTHER**. *He touches her shoulder.)*

It's okay.

DANI. I'm ready.

MARTY.

NOT EVEN DEATH COULD EVER TAKE…

DANI.

YOU FROM ME.

MARTY.

YOU FROM ME.

BOTH.

YOU FROM ME.

(A bright light hits **DANI**.*)*

GOD.

AND SO I OFFER THIS PRAYER:
THE WORLD IS CRUEL, THE WORLD IS UNFAIR.
BUT YOU'LL FIND HOPE LIVES EVERYWHERE,
BENEATH THE GRIEF AND DESPAIR.

*(***GOD*** covers* **MOTHER***'s eyes.)*

GOD. *(cont.)*

REQUIEM, NOW PAIN SHALL CEASE.
REQUIEM…

*(***GOD*** removes his hand.* **MOTHER** *sees* **DANI**.*)*

MOTHER. Danica.

*(***MARTY*** helps* **DANI** *take off her hat. Her hair falls down on her shoulders.)*

GOD.

IN ETERNAL PEACE.

(The lights fade on **GOD** *and* **MOTHER**. *They linger on* **DANI** *and* **MARTY** *for a moment. They lock pinkies and laugh softly. The lights fade to black.)*